W9-BYK-953

THE FAMOUS NINI

A Mostly True Story of
How a Plain White Cat Became a Star

by Mary Nethery

Illustrated by John Manders

CLARION BOOKS
Houghton Mifflin Harcourt
Boston * New York
2010

Clarion Books
215 Park Avenue South
New York, New York 10003
Text copyright © 2010 by Mary Nethery
Illustrations copyright © 2010 by John Manders
The illustrations were executed in gouache
and colored pencil.
The text was set in 14-point Sabon.

Clarion Books is an imprint of Houghton Mifflin Harcourt Publishing Company.

www.hmhbooks.com

Manufactured in China

Library of Congress Cataloging-in-Publication Data

Nethery, Mary.
The famous Nini : a mostly true story of how a plain white cat became a star /
by Mary Nethery ; illustrated by John Manders.
p. cm.
ISBN: 978-0-618-97769-7
Summary: In Venice, Italy, in the 1890s, a stray cat draws attention to a coffee shop in
   which he inspired composer Giuseppe Verdi, and as the feline's fame grows, the shop's
      owner entertains royalty, the pope, and many others. Includes historical notes about
         the real Nini and his visitors.
            1. Verdi, Giuseppe, 1813–1901—Fiction. 2. Fame—Fiction. 3. Cats—Fiction.
               4. Coffee shops—Fiction. 5. Venice (Italy)—History—1866—Fiction.
                  6. Italy—History—1870–1914—Fiction. I. Manders, John. II. Title
                     PZ7.N4388 Fam 2009
                        E22   2008043691

LEO 10 9 8 7 6 5 4 3 2 1

4500208418

To my nonna Teresa and my nonna Anita;
my father, Gino; my mother, Helen, who loves all things Italian;
and to my beloveds, Han and H.A.
—M.N.

Per le mie italiane ragazze bellissime, Gianna ed Andrea.
—J.M.

$\mathcal{L}$ONG ago in Venice, on the Piazza San Marco, Nonna Framboni owned a *caffè*. She served strong coffee and sweet treats. But the *caffè* was so small, people passed by as if it didn't exist.

One afternoon, Nonna opened the door, hoping the scent of coffee might bring in a customer. There sat a plain white cat. "Nini the stray," said Nonna. "Every day you beg on the piazza. Now I find you at my door. But I have no food to spare, not even a scrap."

Moments later, a man entered the *caffè*. Nini followed close behind.

As Nonna served the man coffee, she saw that he was writing musical notes on paper.

"How is it that I, Verdi, must struggle to find the right note?" he muttered, scribbling wildly.

Nonna crossed herself in surprise. Her customer was Giuseppe Verdi, the famous composer!

Verdi pounded his fist on the table in frustration.

Nini meowed.

"Ah, puss!" Verdi cried. "You have given me the exact note I need!"

He danced around the *caffè* with Nini in his arms.

The next morning, Nonna put an announcement in
the window: THE GREAT VERDI TAKES HIS COFFEE HERE.
Maybe this will bring in a few customers, she thought.

It worked. Soon people crowded into the *caffè*, hoping to see Verdi. At noon, he returned. "Where is the singing cat?" he demanded.

"Nini the stray?" Nonna asked.

"Nini the extraordinary!" Verdi gushed. "He gave me a priceless gift. In return, I bring him a line of music from my opera *La Traviata*." Verdi whisked a slip of lined paper from his pocket.

At just that moment, Nini trotted into the *caffè*—
and dropped a mouse at Verdi's feet.

The crowd roared with laughter.

"Ah, puss! Another gift!" Verdi cried. "For this, I shall
dedicate my next opera to you!" He held Nini on high for
all to admire.

The crowd cheered. *"Bravissimo! Bravissimo!"*

That evening, her pockets full of coins, Nonna put up another sign:
SEE THE FAMOUS NINI HERE.

"Nini, my stray," she said. "I know you are just a cat, but this might bring even more customers." She set a saucer of cream on the doorstep. Nini wrapped his tail around her leg.

News spread quickly. Soon artisans came to compare their glass beads to Nini's eyes, hoping for a perfect match. Poets sat with Nini for inspiration. Noblemen told stories about him in the palace halls.

Then one day the king and queen of Italy arrived at the packed *caffè*. They approached Nini, who sat on a table, accepting treats from customers.

"We have a royal disagreement only you can rule upon,"
the queen said to Nini.

"On Saint Anthony's Day," said the king, "the queen wishes
to serve stewed plums for dessert. I vote for creamy pudding."

"Yummy plums?" asked the queen.

Nini twitched one ear.

"Or luscious creamy pudding?" asked the king.

Nini licked his lips.

"I win!" the king shouted, jumping up and down.
"I proclaim tomorrow National Nini Day!"
"*Mamma mia!*" said Nonna.

Later, when the *caffè* closed for
the night, she added another sign:
CELEBRATE NATIONAL NINI DAY HERE.

"Nini, my almond,"
she said. "Won't you stay
and sleep by the fire?"
Nini stretched out on the
hearth, and Nonna petted him
until his fur glistened.

On National Nini Day, people danced, ate creamy pudding, and tossed rose petals. Then came a big surprise.

The pope himself arrived!

"Your Holiness!" Nonna bowed her head and crossed herself.

"Where is this famous Nini that everyone is talking about?" asked the pope.

Nonna presented Nini.

The pope smiled. "Blessings be on Nini, who gives such joy," he said. He raised his hand.

Nini raised his paw. He patted the pope's shiny ring.

The pope's smile grew into a wide grin. "Can it be?" he said. "Has Nini just blessed the pope?"

No one had ever seen him so amused. The crowd cheered with thunderous applause.

When the revelers left, Nonna added a new sign: NINI BLESSES POPE AND MAKES HIM SMILE.

"Maybe I've been exaggerating a bit," Nonna said to Nini, "but what can it hurt?" She made minestrone, and they dined by firelight. Then she fell asleep in her chair, with Nini curled up at her feet.

After the pope's blessing, Nini's fame spread to the far ends of the earth. On the eve of Carnivale, the czar of Russia sent a gift addressed to "The Noble Nini."

Inside the box was a jeweled egg. Inside the egg was a silver mouse. Inside the mouse, a silver bird. And inside the bird, a golden fish. Never had Nonna seen such treasure. She displayed the exquisite egg in the front window, along with another announcement: CZAR DECLARES NINI NOBLE.

Nonna held Nini in her arms as they basked in the beauty of the stunning egg. "Nini, my fig," she said. "I am so happy!"

On the first day of Carnivale, Nonna baked pastries stuffed with apricot jam and dusted with powdered sugar. She had never before been able to buy such expensive ingredients as these. Her customers dressed in fancy costumes and masks. Even Nini wore a mask.

That afternoon, Verdi appeared with an urgent message. "Tonight the emperor of Ethiopia is coming to Carnivale to see Nini," he said. "He seeks Nini's help. He needs a miracle."

For the longest time, Nonna held Nini in her lap. "I love you, my little cannoli," she said. "But you cannot work miracles. When this night is over, everyone will remember you're just a cat. An ordinary stray cat. What will become of us then?" She began to cry.

That evening, Verdi brought the emperor and his daughter to the *caffè*. Nonna sat them at the best table by the fire. She offered pastries on her prettiest plate. The child, in her father's lap, took a bite but said nothing.

"My daughter, Zewditu, has not spoken since her mother died," said the emperor, his eyes dark pools of sadness. "That is why I have come to see the famous Nini. Surely a cat who can help Verdi find the right note, who can settle a royal argument, who can cause the pope himself to smile, can get my Zewditu to speak."

Nonna gasped. "Please, Your Highness, forgive my exaggerations." She crossed herself. "Those were wondrous things, but not truly of the cat's making. My Nini is just an ordinary stray."

Hearing his name, Nini sprang to the table. He went straight to Zewditu, who clung to her father.

"She is afraid," said the emperor. "She has never been near a cat before."

Nonna removed Nini's mask. "See? He's just a kitty," she said.

Nini stepped closer.

Zewditu shrank back.

Nini stretched out and licked a bit of sugar from the tip of her nose.

Zewditu stared at Nini. Then she touched his forehead.

Nini tiptoed into her lap and leaned against her chest.

Zewditu laid her head on his.

Nini purred.

"Father!" she whispered.

"He makes the sound of angels."

Tears ran down the emperor's cheeks. "My Zewditu speaks," he said. "The famous Nini has performed a miracle." He hugged his daughter. He hugged Nini.

Nonna leaned down and kissed Nini's round cheeks. "Oh, wonderful, marvelous, extraordinary cat!" she exclaimed.

"We must celebrate!" Verdi declared. "Everyone—
to my new opera!"

For the first time ever, Nonna Framboni took the evening off,
and a cat was seen at the opera—in the best seat in the house!

29

Late that night, under a sprinkling of stars and powdered sugar, Nonna tucked Nini into her shawl. "Nini, my cream puff," she said, holding him close. "Isn't life as sweet as pastry?"

Nini closed his eyes and purred.

NINI AND HIS FANS

An Author's Note

Nini   Nini was a plain white tom cat who lived in a *caffè*, or coffee shop, in Venice in the 1890s and became a national celebrity. Calling upon Nini and signing his guest book was the thing to do. When Nini died, many important people paid tribute to him. He was called "a rare gem" and "a gentleman, white of fur, and affable with great and small."

No one knows *why* Nini became such a star. So I asked myself the question "What does a cat have to offer that no other creature possesses?" The answer? A purr, one of the most primal and soothing sounds in the universe, a gift that only a cat can give. That's what led to this story. All of the notable visitors were real people who came to see Nini, but the events in the story didn't unfold in the same way that I have presented them.

Nonna Framboni   According to one source, the *caffè* was owned by a man named Antonio Panciera. But since I have a *nonna,* an Italian grandmother, I created Nonna Framboni.

Giuseppe Verdi   The composer actually wrote a few notes from *La Traviata* in Nini's visitors book. Most of Verdi's operas are tragedies. But his last, *Falstaff,* performed during Nini's lifetime, is a comedy. I imagined that Verdi considered dedicating an opera to Nini, and surely he would have chosen a comedy.

King Umberto I and Queen Margherita of Italy   The royal couple *did* come to call on Nini, and they signed his book. It's fun to suppose they had a royal squabble for him to settle.

Pope Leo XIII   It's reasonable to think that the pope blessed Nini when he came to visit him at the *caffè*. After all, Pope Leo was the patron of the French Society for the Prevention of Cruelty to Animals.

Nini's Caffè Dei Frari, in present-day Venice.

Czar Alexander III In the Russian Orthodox Church, Easter is celebrated with the exchanging of eggs and three kisses. In 1885, the czar had the first Fabergé egg made as an Easter gift for his wife. It is now called the Hen Egg. Even though it is made of gold and enamel, it looks like a plain white egg. But when it is opened, a "golden" yolk is found, and inside the yolk is a golden hen, and inside the hen is a ruby crown and a pendant (now lost). There were 105 Fabergé eggs made by Peter Carl Fabergé between 1885 and 1917. So I imagined that when the czar came to call on Nini, he gave the cat a Fabergé egg, too.

Emperor Menelik II The emperor of Ethiopia did, indeed, come to see Nini. It's not known if his daughter, Zewditu, accompanied him. But if she did, she probably wouldn't have been familiar with cats. They were not considered appropriate pets for Ethiopian royalty and were more likely to be found in villages.

Zewditu Emperor Menelik's daughter was very young when her mother died, and I loved the idea of a cat's simple purr bringing her comfort. She was known for being kind to everyone she met, royalty and servants alike. When she grew up, she was proclaimed Empress, Queen of Kings, and was the first woman to sit on the Ethiopian imperial throne since the Queen of Sheba.

32